SHERLOCK HOLMES

The Adventure of the Deadly Illusion

RON BRACKIN

Author of the *New York Times* bestseller, *Son of Hamas*

Additional Titles

- Son of Hamas
- The Prophetic Path
- The Power and Victory of Communion
- MindShift
- A closer look at Love
- Have You Lost Your Mind?
- The Bold & Conquering Power of Faith
- Night at the George W. Bush Presidential Museum
- Chats with my Beloved
- Much Ado about Nothing: A Devotional
- Dracula: A Devotional
- Oliver Twist: A Devotional

Contents

Preface

I met Mrs. Alice Bedinfield at what I expected to be another rubber-chicken-and-boiled-potato affair on Capitol Hill, where politicians break bread with community leaders and toss off platitudes until the cash bar closes.

The issue *du jour* was homelessness, the unsolvable problem that Washington is certain it could solve if it could just appropriate another hundred billion or so.

As the evening progressed, the guests smiled and nodded, shook congressional hands, and promised their support as they continued to fight for the disenfranchised.

All the guests, that is, except Mrs. Bedinfield.

She wasn't rude or stand-offish. On the contrary, she was gracious and sociable. She just looked too savvy to be there. A smartly dressed, diminutive woman with interested blue eyes, she appeared decades younger than her 82 years.

I introduced myself, and as everyone else was discussing "the issue," we did too. And soon, I discovered a kindred spirit. She spoke of long-forgotten concepts like the "worthy poor, people willing and able to work and who just need a hand up, as opposed to those bred to the dole.

Suddenly, she paused and began to laugh.

"I'm afraid I hold strong opinions in this area, Mr. Brackin. I'm terribly sorry for going on so. Please forgive me.

"I suppose I'm like Mrs. Hilton Cubitt in *The Adventure of the Dancing Men.* Are you familiar with Sherlock Holmes, Mr. Brackin? At the end of that classic tale, Dr. Watson explains that Mrs. Cubitt 'remains a widow, devoting her whole life to the care of the poor and to the administration of her husband's estate.'

"He is my great uncle, you know."

"Who is?"

"John H. Watson, chronicler of Mr. Sherlock Holmes."

I was stunned, and the reception held no further interest. Mrs. Bedinfield and I withdrew to a corner where we talked about Holmes and Watson until the doors closed, then went to Denny's and continued our conversation over a pot of coffee.

The following week, I received an invitation to tea and listened for many more delightful hours to stories about her family and life in England.

Her father was Robert H. Watson, nephew of Dr. John Watson. Her grandfather, the doctor's elder brother, died a drunkard in 1888. His demise is recorded in Sir Arthur Conan Doyle's novel, *The Sign of Four.*

"My father," she said, "was a physician—and a bit of an

adventurer, I'm afraid—like his uncle John. He was sixteen when his father died. To clarify his thoughts and decide what to do with his life, he signed aboard a ship of the great Peninsular and Oriental Line bound for India.

"Two years later, he used his earnings along with a modest inheritance to study medicine and establish a small practice. But Daddy must have heard too many of Uncle's tales and visited too many exotic places, because he was fascinated by aberrant human behavior, drifted irresistibly toward forensic pathology, and until his death in 1955, served as a consultant to New Scotland Yard.

"It didn't pay much and left little time to develop his own practice, but he loved the work and was very happy."

During another visit, Mrs. Bedinfield brought out a leather document case containing a typed manuscript, a gift from her father just before his death. She asked that I take it home, read it and bring it back the following day.

Included was a letter from her father, dated February 12, 1955, which read:

Dearest Alice,

> How delightful to hear that you and Roger are coming to visit. I only wish you were able to stay longer and that Roger had less business to attend to across the Channel. I am

thoroughly enjoying playing host in what you persist in referring to as my retirement. Yet, I have never been busier and, between visitors, I keep quite occupied, thank you, with occasional calls from the Yard, requesting an opinion on this or that. Of course, modern criminology has expanded well beyond my abilities to keep pace, but there still seems to be a place for common sense amongst the clever gadgets and gauges used to analyze crime-scene evidence today.

Do you remember my mentioning Dr. John Newell, the Australian entomologist who provided such valuable assistance in the Gerrish murder investigation several years ago? Well, Newell and his wife, Marjorie, were my houseguests last week.

A confirmed bibliophile, she was anxious to browse the Charing Cross bookstalls, so John and I visited St. Bartholomew's Hospital. I showed him the plaque that commemorates my uncle's introduction to Holmes in the chem lab, and would you believe it, John's an absolutely rabid fan and was amazed to learn of our kinship to the master detective—or at the least, to his Boswell.

As I was saying, that evening I took John and

Marjorie to the S.H. Pub & Restaurant for a bit of roast beef and Yorkshire pudding. As we sat looking into the full-size replica of the Baker St. sitting room, I found myself thinking about some of the pre-Watsonian adventures that took place during Holmes's first term at Oxford.

Uncle John told me those stories as Holmes told them to him. I suppose they stand out in my mind because most took place the year I was born and involve the Rev. Charles L. Dodgson, a mathematics lecturer at Christ Church, who wrote the delightful Wonderland books under the pen name of Lewis Carroll.

Dodgson, you may recall, was Holmes's don. As we know, he cared little for undergraduates nor they for him. In fact, he had an aversion to boys, preferring the cheery company of young girls—all, of course, aboveboard and beyond any hint of impropriety. Holmes too was unique. And the two shared diverse interests, including crime, the theatre and science. Both were raised in Yorkshire, you know—Dodgson at the Croft Rectory and Holmes at the farmstead in the North Riding.

But I suspect it was Holmes's master of logic and observation that most intrigued Dodgson. He was never able to devise a mathematical code, game or puzzle that Holmes could not decipher or unravel.

While you've heard many of the early stories about Holmes and Dodgson, there is one I've never told you. Therefore, I began this weekend to write down for you, hopefully with uncle's precision and attention to detail, the facts surrounding one of the first and most incredible cases Sherlock Holmes would ever encounter.

And now, dearest Alice, I shall end my letter and continue my new project in hope that I will have concluded by the time you and Roger arrive in the spring.

With all my love …

The next morning, Mrs. Bedinfield asked if I would consider grooming her father's manuscript into a short book or novella. It was a special story to him, she said, and had special significance to her as well, though she never said what.

I agreed. And what you are about to read is the account of the case that virtually set the stage for the amazing career of the world's first consulting detective.

The first case

JULY 1898. For the seventh time, Holmes crossed the room and stood at the window staring into the sodden world of Baker Street. He sighed heavily and ground his teeth in time with his dark thoughts. The rain had fallen for three days with neither respite nor tempest to ease the monotony.

Worst of all, Holmes had completed his last case nearly two weeks earlier, a burglary made challenging only by the ineptness of the burglar. What had appeared to be a clever deception had proved to be no more than a clumsy mistake which, once recognized, made the villain's capture absurdly simple. It was a solution for which Holmes encouraged Gregson to claim all the credit and which the Scotland Yard inspector humbly did.

Newspapers were strewn about the floor around Holmes's chair. Only a few had holes marking the absence of a few articles of moderate interest. Suddenly, he spun around, threw up his hands and shouted, "Watson, I surrender! I am entirely bankrupt and devoid of hope."

And without another word, he poured a tumbler of whiskey, splashed in soda from the gasogene, and folded his long frame into the armchair.

Setting his drink on the table, he shoved a plug of shag

tobacco into the bowl of his old briar and was soon sipping whiskey and drawing deeply on his pipe with his eyes closed. Slowly, a slight smirk crossed his lips, and he waved his hand as if interrupting a memory. His eyes opened.

"Apparently, the entire London underworld is as subdued as we are by this devilish downpour. Therefore, since they are intent on providing us no occupation—and if you will set aside what I am certain must be an enlightening issue of the *Lancet*—I will give you the account of a case I have never mentioned and one which you may one day craft into yet another titillating tale for *The Strand*."

He closed his eyes, and the doctor saw that his mind was already reliving some earlier adventure that, although its telling was a poor substitute for a fresh challenge, would ease the torpor and help pass the evening quite pleasantly after all.

Watson put down the magazine, although the article he had been reading was indeed of considerable interest to him, poured a drink, lit his pipe and settled onto the sofa with a notepad and pencil.

After one more reflective pull on his pipe, Holmes set it aside, touched the tips of his fingers together, and rested his head against the back of the chair.

The enigmatic academic

IT WAS SUNDAY, September 29, 1872, Holmes' initial year at Christ Church.

The first month of the long vacation, he had spent at Donnithorpe, in Norfolk, with Victor Trevor, the only friend he made at Oxford among the men of his year.

He was engaged in his first case which would end with the sudden death of Trevor's father and the disclosure of the grim history of the *Gloria Scott*.

During the months that followed his visit to Donnithorpe, Holmes remained mostly in his London rooms working out private experiments in organic chemistry—Oxford, being keener on the classics than on applied science.

On frequent occasions, he enjoyed the assistance of the Rev. Charles Lutwidge Dodgson, a brilliant mathematician, albeit a tedious lecturer.

Dodgson was an enigma. His stiff posture belied the lithe, Puckish elf within, and a mop of curly hair clashed with his impeccable dress.

At The House, a popular nickname for Christ Church, he was the consummate academician and cleric, somber, dignified and priggish.

Yet, one could enter his rooms to find him crawling on his hands and knees, tossing his shaggy mane and roaring like a beast to amuse a child guest, of whom there were many and frequent, all eager subjects for his camera. For he was an accomplished photographer whose notable subjects included many of England's finest artists, scientists and scholars, as well as several crowned heads.

Despite his austere reputation as a member of the deaconate, Dodgson was an inveterate patron of the theatre, and he and Holmes were that evening returning from the Egyptian Hall in Piccadilly.

Predictably, Dodgson's childlike fascination with magic, indeed any trick, toy or invention, had got the best of him.

"I was confounded, Holmes," said he, "from the moment Jasper exploded onto the stage in a flash of lightning and a cloud of red smoke, and I've no doubt that I shall go raving trying to reckon how he subsequently managed to furnish a bare stage from thin air."

Though a superlative logician, Dodgson preferred to set aside his deductive talents when he attended the theatre and allow himself to be manipulated into seeing only what he was meant to see and into believing what he was led to believe. He loved fantasy and nonsense, but while master of both, chose to be their consumer as well as their creator.

"Perhaps I can offer some illumination," said Holmes.

"Tell me what you saw through your eyes of wonder, and through the eyes of logic, I'll tell you what actually took place."

Staring at the wall of their carriage as though it had been transformed into the Egyptian Hall, Dodgson became more and more animated as he reviewed each movement and once again experienced the wonder of the performance.

"After the smoke cleared a bit, Jasper looked about him at the empty stage, then at the audience, shrugging his shoulders as though surprised that someone had neglected to set out his furniture and props. Continuing in pantomime as the orchestra struck a waltz, he strolled to the prompt side and with a broad sweep of his arm, caused to appear a slender crystal table. The wizard bowed to the table, and a large oriental vase filled with living flowers materialized."

Dodgson's excitement threatened to trigger his familiar stammer.

"Walking confidently about the stage, Jasper made heavy wooden tables, tall brass lampstands, plush divans, massive marble sculptures, busts and pedestals, and a great wicker cage filled with exotic, squawking birds to appear at his command until the entire area was richly furnished."

"Wonderful, my friend!" said Holmes, applauding. "You described it precisely as the conjuror intended that you should.

7

Your profound mystery, however, is easily explained."

"Eliminate the impossible and whatever remains no matter how improbable must be the solution?"

"Precisely. Guided by my axiom, then, we clearly eliminate sleight-of-hand. What you saw was not accomplished like so many cups and balls, palmed and secreted in hidden pockets; these were obviously solid, weighty, pieces.

"What remains is that the furnishings did not come onto the stage out of concealment but rather that the concealment was removed to reveal the furnishings. All the furniture was already on the stage, hidden from our view, when Jasper made his entrance. How, then, was it hidden and where?

"The only concealment that will answer is one that the eye is unable to distinguish from the background—like black velvet, the pile of which absorbs reflection.

"Once we know precisely where to focus our attention, we easily observe the barely perceptible movement of an assistant in a hooded black costume and gloves—an invisible pair of hands imperceptibly following the conjuror about the stage, and on cue, snatching away the draperies which covered the furnishings, making them seem to appear from nowhere, *et voilà!*"

"Bravo, Holmes!"

"Quite elementary, old man, really. But sometimes I envy

your ability to lose yourself in these amusements. My mind, I'm afraid, habitually resists misdirection and is satisfied only by searching out methods, motives and means."

"Your analytical skills are formidable, Holmes," said Dodgson, goading his friend into exposing another secret. "but I don't believe that even you could have seen behind every illusion. The floating young woman. Undoubtedly, that one has you stumped."

Convinced that Dodgson would be far happier with his mysteries left intact than with a lesson in the methods of Hindu fakirs, Holmes left him to his ruminations until the train arrived at Oxford Station.

The rain, having stopped by the time they reached the archway at Tom Quad, its air heavy with the smell of ancient stones and wet grass, the two returned silently to their rooms, each absorbed in his own thoughts—Dodgson still puzzling over The Magnificent Jasper's illusions and Holmes eager to resume his study of tobacco ash.

Holmes was savoring an aromatic Latakian when a loud pounding erupted.

When he opened the door, Dodgson rushed past, handing off a note and pacing the floor while Holmes read:

PRITCHARD MURDERED STOP JEWELS STOLEN STOP COME IMMEDIATELY STOP BRING HOLMES

"An ugly business, Dodgson. But why is he reaching out to us instead of Scotland Yard?"

"Sir Arthur Bellingham is a fellow member of the Reform Club. During a recent game of cards, I told him how you convinced the police of the innocence of young James Gaffney in the Bishopgate jewel case. I suppose he hopes we might be of assistance to him."

"Let's see then."

Death and magic

UPON ARRIVING AT SYDENHAM HILL STATION, they found a carriage waiting to take them to Highstone Manor. A constable at the front door of the Manor had been instructed to admit them, and the housekeeper led them directly to the library.

Holmes and Dodgson entered a room crowded with stout leather chairs grouped around a long desk of black walnut. Thick tapestries, heavily-framed portraiture and dark, stormy seascapes covered the paneled walls. Behind the desk, bookcases flanked a huge stone fireplace.

The only access to the library was from the entry hall or through the French doors that led to the garden.

"It's good of you to come, Dodgson. This must be Mr. Sherlock Holmes.

"Chief Inspector Jenkins," said Sir Arthur Bellingham, turning to a broad, ruddy-featured man, "I sent for these gentlemen in the hope that they might be of some assistance."

"That was thoughtful of you, sir, I'm sure," said the officer. "But this is police business and a simple case. I don't expect we'll be needing outside assistance.

"It's obvious that the burglar came in through those doors by cutting a hole in the glass of one side, then reaching in and unlocking the other side. While he was stealing the jewels, your man came in and caught him in the act. They struggled, the burglar stabbed him and left the way he came. We'll have him when we find your jewels."

Across the room, the doctor finished his examination of the body and was about to remove the murder weapon.

"Wait!" shouted Holmes, running to the corpse, which was on its side obstructing one of the doors. Its features were frozen in an expression of surprise.

"Here, what are you doing?" said Jenkins. "I told you this is police business. Move away from there!"

"I believe I saw something," Chief Inspector, "that might help you solve your mystery."

"There is no mystery, Mr. Holmes. It's all very simple. The burglar was seen breaking in, and we were sent for. We must have arrived just as he was struggling with the butler. He panicked, stabbed the butler and ran for it. There's no important evidence to be missed. Let's finish up here, men.

"I'll take that, doctor."

The murder weapon was curiously-tooled steel. One end was tapered into an ugly point; the other looked remarkably like a skeleton key with a sturdy barb attached to the shaft by a snug-fitting ring which could slide to the far end of the shaft and lock in place.

"What do you make of this, Sir Arthur?" asked Jenkins. "Ever seen it before?"

"No, I can't imagine what it is."

"Notice the lint snagged in the bitting of the key, Chief Inspector," Holmes suggested. "Whoever killed Pritchard had to wrap a cloth round the end to avoid damaging his hand as he gripped the weapon tightly enough to drive it home— clearly not the the way the instrument was meant to be used."

"Yes, I'll be sure to take that into account, Mr. Holmes. ... Alright, you two, don't just stand there. Let's go."

The officers removed the body, with Jenkins behind.

"Well, I suppose that's that," said Sir Arthur. "I am sorry to have brought you two out here for nothing."

"Not at all, Sir Arthur. Despite the Chief Inspector's assurance, this is far from the simple case he believes it to be. In fact, it is not a common burglary at all."

"What do you mean, Holmes?"

"I mean, my friend, that we have a far more intriguing mystery before us now than any of your Egyptian Hall tricks. "But first," he said, turning to Sir Arthur, "we need to know precisely what happened this evening."

"Of course, gentlemen. Please, sit down. Let me offer you a drink and a fill for your pipes." He rang for a servant.

"I suppose I should begin with the jewels. There were three matched pieces—a tiara, necklace and a ring, set with diamonds and rubies. Old family pieces. My wife never wears them. Afraid they'll be lost or someone will steal them. They're kept in a vault at Holder & Stevenson in the City. But we're expected at a reception at Buckingham, and that helped Judith overcome her anxiety.

"Yes, well, yesterday I drove to London personally and brought the jewels here to Highstone."

Sir Arthur rose, walked to the bookcase at the right of the fireplace and removed several large volumes, revealing a small wall safe.

"I was certain they would be secure here until after the reception. But when Judith and I returned from Covent Garden tonight, well, you see now exactly what I saw when I came to get a book before retiring."

"Not exactly, Sir Arthur. You just removed the books in front of the safe. Were they in place when you came down?"

"Why, no, Mr. Holmes, they were not. They were stacked neatly at the corner of my desk. I thought the maid must have replaced them on the shelf. Out of habit, I suppose. Ellen is a compulsive tidier, a gem to have when one wants things neat but rather annoying if you've set something out intentionally."

"Did anyone know of your invitation to Buckingham and that your wife intended to wear the jewels?"

"No one except Judith and a few of the fellows at the club."

"I see."

With Sir Arthur's permission, Holmes examined the room. Then, as it was very late, they bade their host goodnight and promised to keep him informed of their progress.

"Come, Dodgson, we must return to the Egyptian Hall," Holmes said when they arrived at Sydenham Hill Station. "I believe you told me your friend Maskelyne has been virtually living in his workshop creating some sensational new illusion. If so, we have need of his unique skills."

Headed once again for Piccadilly, Holmes asked Dodgson to draw a detailed sketch of the unusual tool used to murder Robert Pritchard.

"Do you remember Alexander Herrmann and his Sing Sing illusion, Dodgson? Though the method is childishly simple, it provides an insight into the real life illusion before us.

"I'm not sure I understand."

"It involves a double hoax. You'll recall that there were two prison cells at the ends of the stage, barred on all four sides. Atop each side appeared to be a rolled, red shade. Behind them was a curtain painted to look like a stone wall.

"Herrmann walked completely around the left cell to demonstrate that it was empty. Then, he passed in front of the right cell. Suddenly, there was a commotion offstage.

"'Stop him! He's escaped!' someone shouted. And a convict in a striped prison uniform ran onto the stage with manacles dangling from one wrist.

"Herrmann pulled out a pistol, arrested the convict and forced him into the right-hand cell. Clanging the steel door shut and locking it, he circled the cell and pulled down the shades, front to back.

"As he did so, a voice from inside began shouting, 'Let me out! Let me out!'

"Immediately, he raised the shades again, revealing a prison guard instead of a convict.

"Just then, a shout went up at the back of the theatre, and the manacled convict rushed past us onto the stage.

By then, Herrmann had released the guard, and both of them grabbed the convict, forced him into the cell on the left and quickly drew the shades on both cells.

"Herrmann coolly aimed his revolver at the cell holding the convict and fired. The blinds flew up, and the convict was gone again.

"Then Herrmann spun around, fired at the other cell, up went the blinds and we saw the convict angrily shaking the bars. Do you see, Dodgson?"

"I see nothing but an impossible feat."

"Not at all. The back shade of each cell was painted exactly like the grey stone background behind it.

"Behind the camouflage shade of the right-hand cell, an assistant waited, dressed as the guard.

"When Hermann put the convict into the cell and drew down the three red shades, the assistant drew up the camouflage shade, switched places with the convict through a set of flexible bars and drew down the camouflage shade once again. Are you following me, Dodgson?

"Why, this is too easy, Holmes."

"Of course. The most obvious is rarely suspect. Now, as soon as the guard was revealed, it was the cue for a second convict, dressed like the first, to run down the aisle. He was then placed in the left cell."

"I see."

"Then, when Herrmann drew the red shades of this cell, the duplicate convict slipped out through the loose bars, drew down the camouflage shade and hid behind it. The original convict then stepped back into the right cell from behind the camouflage shade. Herrmann fired his pistol. An empty cell was revealed on the left. Then, he fired again and revealed the convict back in the right-hand cell."

"Incredible! And so simple once I saw the principle."

"The point is that, just as there were actually two convicts at the Egyptian Hall … there were two burglars at Highstone."

"How on earth do you deduce that?"

"You did not draw the same conclusions merely because you did not make the same observations. When we entered Highstone, I looked for evidence of forced entry on the brass plate of the front door but found none. So it was logical, as Jenkins concluded, that the burglar had broken in through the French doors in the library, since they were the only other way in. And, in fact, one of the burglars almost did. But not the murderer.

"When I examined the hole that had been cut in the glass, I observed glass dust on the frame of the window pane. The frame, of course, was beveled downward, so some of the glass dust would have to have fallen on the floor directly beneath the hole. But, when I looked, I found it on the butler's coat, which meant he was murdered before the hole was cut.

"Next, I saw that Sir Arthur's wall safe requires two keys to open, and there was no evidence of forced entry, indicating that the burglar probably had assistance from a member of the household. A highly placed servant would be the most likely to have access to the keys.

"You may also recall that Sir Arthur said the books were stacked on the corner of his desk when he entered the room. A burglar would not waste precious time to be neat, nor would he be the least bit concerned about mistreating his victim's books by throwing them on the floor.

"The suspicion, therefore, fell upon Pritchard. But, as yet, there is no evidence against him.

"Nevertheless, let us say that Pritchard had let in the burglar through the front door and opened the safe for him. Why then was he killed? To keep him quiet?"

"I think not, Holmes," said Dodgson, warming to the challenge. "What threat could the butler be? If he was caught, his participation would earn him the same sentence as the burglar."

"Indeed, Dodgson, there might have been a falling out among thieves, but that would not explain the call to the police and the arrival of the second burglar through the library doors.

"No, Pritchard's murder was neither an accident of fate nor an act of passion. It was a component of a dark plan.

"Remember the lint in the murder weapon, which I pointed out to our level-headed Chief Inspector? I concluded for him that a cloth handle was not the tool's natural state, but he was uninterested, so I kept it to myself. In fact, these tiny threads have much more to reveal.

"For example, had the crime taken place as Jenkins supposes, we would be forced to believe that the burglar, suddenly surprised by Pritchard, grabbed this tool, looked about for something to wrap around it to protect his hands and struggled with the butler, who was waiting patiently for his murderer to prepare his weapon.

"Once engaged, the murderer stabbed the butler and left behind this highly unusual and presumably incriminating tool for the police to trace.

"That won't do. That said, what do the threads tell us?

"First, the weapon was not wrapped as an afterthought in the heat of battle but beforehand and deliberately. Since it is impossible that the murderer could have been surprised by the butler, he must have known the butler would be there, and he must have intended to kill him all along. Then, he intentionally left behind the weapon to lead the police to its owner—the second burglar.

"We will know no more until we find that man, Dodgson. And I am confident we shall do so through the tool you have so accurately drawn. But as excellent as your artistic

22

talents are, the work ahead needs something more substantial.

"And so, to Maskelyne for a late night favor."

Groats and grunters

STANDING LIKE a massive granite pyramid between the chemists and the Dudley Gallery was the Egyptian Hall, two huge undraped statues towering above its doors and supported by four stone columns.

Inside, red lacquered walls were covered with illustrated posters promising supernatural feats of mystical wizardry:

THE GREAT HERRMANN
and his amazing specialities!
DECAPITATION!
The SPIRIT CABINET!
Every Day at 3 & 8. Marvelous Changes!
Illusions & Surprises!

HELLER'S WONDERS!
SECOND SIGHT!
ANTI-SPIRITIST DEMONSTRATIONS!
Illusions & Pianologues!

Exhibits of escapist paraphernalia—manacles and shackles unable to restrain guest conjurors, an oak trunk bound with heavy chains and brass padlocks, razor-edged swords thrust through a sarcophagus (with crimson paint daubed along the business ends)—all displayed to prepare the spectator for what he would see, or imagine he saw, on stage.

Holmes and Dodgson went to the front doors and knocked. Receiving no response, they tried the alley and rang the bell at the stage door.

"Who the devil is it?" thundered a voice inside after the third ring. "What do you want?"

Suddenly, John Nevil Maskelyne swung open the door, his shirtsleeves rolled to the elbows and his leather apron flecked with oil and shimmering metal shavings.

"Good heavens, Dodgson! What brings you abroad at this ungodly hour? Come in. Come in. What made you think I would be here? Or is it me you're looking for?"

"This is my friend, Mr. Sherlock Holmes, a bit of a wizard himself, although his gift is more sleight of mind than sleight of hand. And yes, you are indeed the one we're looking for.

"When last we met, I asked you to pose for my camera, and you said a new mechanical experiment was absorbing all of your time. I thought we might find you working late."

"Yes, of course. Well, I'm pleased to meet you, Mr. Holmes. Come along. Forgive me for not taking you upstairs to my office, but it is also my workshop and, well, I'm sure you understand. I'll just bring up the house lights, and we'll sit out here in the theatre while you explain what brings you out in the middle of the night in search of a magician."

"Nothing less than murder, my friend."

After retelling the events, Dodgson handed Maskelyne the sketch he had drawn.

"What do you make of it?"

"Extraordinary! At first glance, it appears to be a cracksman's tool. Conjurors use similar instruments to make their escapes. But I've never seen anything quite like this.

"It's not a common tool like those they make up in Birmingham. The man who owns this is a specialist. What they call a 'snoozer,' I should think. An unusual type of burglar who robs hotel rooms.

"Unlike the chap who burgles houses, the snoozer needs only a couple of tools. See here, at this end, obviously a skeleton key. Hotel locks are absurdly uncomplicated. Too expensive to fit so many doors with sound locks, I suppose. And this little hook slides down to the end like this and locks in place to offer a quite serviceable outsider. He uses that when the guest has turned his key and left it in the lock."

Maskelyne took a warded key out of his pocket.

"You see, the burglar just slips the outsider into the keyhole, comes alongside the butt end of the inside key like this, and turns it back around to unlock the door. But I can imagine no use a snoozer would have for the other end.

"Unless … wait a minute."

He vaulted onto the stage and off to the dressing rooms backstage, then quickly returned.

"I think I can show you its twin if you like."

Maskelyne jumped off the stage carrying a walking stick. With a flourish, he drew out a long, narrow sword, the hilt of which was the handle of the cane.

"My guess is that your murder weapon is actually part of this snoozer's tool kit and that it once had a handle here and the other end fitted into a walking stick. Quite clever."

"I was counting on that," said Holmes. "It will make it easier to find its owner. But a sketch won't answer. I must have the actual tool or one exactly like it. The original is in the care of Scotland Yard, but my friend Dodgson has a high regard for your skill as a smith."

"And you want me to make you a duplicate."

"If you would."

"I'll start now if it will help put a rope around the neck of your murderer any quicker."

"The owner of this tool is not the murderer. But he is quite likely to have the answers that will explain the circumstances surrounding this most uncommon crime.

"Dodgson, I suggest that you return to the House and get some sleep. We have a great deal of work ahead of us. While our friend interrupts the labor of his heart for the cause of justice, I have a few important preparations to make at my rooms."

* * * * *

Dawn was several hours away when Holmes returned to the Egyptian Hall.

"Right on time Mr. Holmes," said Maskelyne as he opened the door, his eyes admiring the newly forged tool in his hands. Then, he looked up.

"What … who are you? What do you want?" The tool suddenly became a weapon, exactly as it had hours before in Bellingham's library.

"I'm terribly sorry to shock you, Mr. Maskelyne. I should have warned you that I'd be sending quite a different man round to pick up that remarkable instrument you have poised to plunge into my chest."

"Mr. Holmes, is that you?" said he. "You're fortunate some constable didn't lock you up on your way over here, skulking about in the middle of the night, looking like you're on the lurk and would strangle a man for tuppence."

"High praise from a master of illusion. I hope I will be as convincing in the rookeries of St. George."

29

The heavy night air soaked through all that it touched. Holmes had visited the West End warrens before and walked their odious alleys many times since, but he could never get past the horror of them, of the contrast between the squalid lodging-houses cringing beneath the gaze of the Palace.

Westminster's ancient towers gaze down at its poor parish. And Parliament's laws hold no sway in the dark, writhing jungle that surrounds its halls.

Holmes's thoughts continued thus throughout the twisting streets and alleyways. And though the night was far spent, the rookery was neither quiet nor idle.

Used women staggered home. Starving children played in the dark with sticks for toys and hissing rats for playmates.

Just ahead was the lodging house he sought.

The air inside was sour. Men and women lay, often thirty and forty to a room, beneath vermin-infested blankets. Some, head to toe, some naked atop the bedding, seeking relief from the lice. All, except those too sodden with hot gin and beer, slept fitfully.

The kitchen was a filthy affair boasting only a fireplace, a greasy wooden table and several worn benches. From a cord stretched across a corner of the room hung two damp shirts and a threadbare pair of breeches.

Holmes went in and held his hands to the coals.

Several men sat at the table. The one they called Rasch was thick and heavy down to his boots. Fierce dark eyes glared out beneath his black brow. His knuckles wore great, hard calluses. A robber rather than a burglar, he favored a cosh over a jimmy.

Rasch overshadowed the skittery hackney driver, Skewes, whose night-time clientele consisted of burglars, coach thieves and grave robbers who paid well for speed and anonymity.

Skewes's eyes caught every movement in the room. He watched as Holmes moved to a corner, sat down and retrieved an apple from his pocket. When Holmes pulled out the snoozer's tool and skewered the fruit, Skewes's eyes darted back and forth from the tool to Rasch like a hound trying to draw its master to a stranger at the gate.

While his eyes twitched thus, his sharp elbow jabbed at the ribs of the third man—a screever, a lawyer's clerk so addicted to gin, self-pity and idleness that he could do nothing to earn his living except forge documents. A mottled opera hat sat at Pruitt's feet as though begging for crumbs. Tied loosely about his throat was a faded yellow belcher.

"Now there's a barmy lookin' chiv," said Skewes, nodding at the tool. "An wot does y'make of it?

"A proper blade for eatin,' says you? Not 'alf, says I. I reckon to 'ave seen sumfin near like it onst before, I think. In the hands of a swell cracksman, I think, who would'n ever be parted from it, lest somebody done him for it."

"Where'd you come by it?" asked Pruitt.

"Found it in the street," said Holmes. "Fancied it."

"Fancies it m'self, I does," said Skewes. "You doesn't know wot it's good for, I'm certain, do y'lad, or y'wouldn't be corin' no apples wi it. But I might have a use for it, if y'druther turn it inta a bit of useful coin, eh?"

"What'll you give for it?"

"Not as much as y'd like, I'm thinkin,' but mor'n yer gettin' out o'it in that there apple.

A groat."

"A shilling."

"Fah! The bloody chiv ain't worth mor'n half a grunter."

"A shilling, or I'll pick my teeth with it."

His eyes screwed down tight and, through a yellow grin, he spat, "Done!" pounding his fist roughly on the table.

Suddenly, he jumped to his feet and jerked the tool out of

32

Holmes' hand.

"My shilling!" said Holmes.

"Your groat!" said he, tossing him a copper and stepping back between his two mates.

Making a show of having been cheated, Holmes heeled it out of the lodging house and into the early morning mist.

There, he waited until Skewes left and followed him through the wakening streets.

After many twists and turns, Skewes turned down a grim, foul-smelling alley and stopped at a barred door.

Holmes watched as he knocked nervously several times, then saw nothing more.

* * * * *

Holmes lay still, his head throbbing. Blood trickled into his ear. He heard four voices. Three belonged to Rasch, Skewes and Pruitt. The fourth was unfamiliar.

"Ow did I know e'd foller me 'ere?"

"That's right, my dear, you was just doin' Solomons a favor, wasn't you?"

A smart blow, and the weasel slunk off whining.

"Let's kill 'im an be done w'it. Yer c'n settle for the cosh an' add a bit to finish the job."

Rasch's voice.

"Patience, my dears. Don't be improodent," said the voice, as it leaned over and sniffed Holmes like a spaniel.

Solomons was a sharp, pointed man. His chin and ears and voice were sharp. His eyes had a glint and an edge to them. Thin shoulders poked through a worn frock coat, and long, slender hands dangled from the sleeves and came to points at his sides.

His back was bent from years of peering through a glass into the fiery hearts of dazzling stones.

"Wot are you doin' there, ol' man?"

He stood upright, cocked his long balding head to one side and laid his finger alongside his nose.

"It don't smell right, my dears. Don't smell right nor look right neither. Don't smell as he belongs here. Smells ratty, it you asks me. Yessss, a young ratty lad that pokes its pointy nose into places where it don't belong, where it don't belong. Skewes!"

The weasel jumped and winced.

"Where did it say it found Strand's skeleton?"

"'E didn't say, just that 'e found it and fancied it."

"Found it and fancied it, I'm sure, my dear. Found it sticking in a corpse and fancied it would lead him to the one what done him, I'm sure.

"Well, we don't have no objections to Strand being nibbed by this young jack, do we, my dears? But it's not Strand's neck alone now, is it? No, now you've led him here. And we can't have young jack telling tales at the Yard and them putting hemp collars around our sweet necks.

"Tie him up, my dears, and let the little river rats pick his pockets at low tide."

The Reform Club

XIE CLIMBED the dark oak staircase from Tom Quad to the new glass-house where she would be transformed into Reynolds's "Penelope Boothby." Her image would then be dipped in pyrogallic acid, rinsed, fixed in a hyposulphate of soda bath, washed, dried and varnished.

Still, young Alexandra Kitchin was not content. Her heart was set on being photographed below in Dodgson's rooms within which were every kind of wonderful amusement. Exotic dolls, a distorting mirror, tiny ivory binoculars which showed photographs of Wonderland's Alice when held toward the light, a juggler tossing balls into the air and a walking bear automaton. Her favorite, however, was "Bob the Bat," an original creation of elastic, gauze and wire that she never tired of winding up and sending flying about the room.

This morning, though, the nine-year-old would be content to imagine herself a queen (she was, after all, god-daughter of Queen Alexandra of Denmark), enthroned atop a majestic mountain and gazing out over her kingdom. Dodgson's roof studio commanded a magnificent view of Oxford, across the Great Quadrangle, past the Meadows to the gentle Isis and nearly as far as Godstow.

Though in his usual playful mood, Dodgson seemed distracted. He took fewer photographs today.

After he had varnished the plates, he ordered refreshments more out of habit and obligation than from a desire to linger in the company of his young friend.

And soon after Xie left, he was on the 10:25 train to London to lunch at his club and try to sort out the events of the previous evening.

* * * * *

The Reform Club was the grandfather of Pall Mall. Ancient, hallowed and stuffy, it suited Dodgson's priggish side and amused his puerile side. In return, he suited and amused the Reform. Dodgson's writings were represented in both of the Club libraries.

The first library, devoted to law, politics and science offered two of his works. The first was *An Elementary Treatise on Determinants with their Application to Simultaneous Linear Equations and Algebraic Geometry.* The second addressed *The Fifth Book of Euclid Treated Algebraically, so far as it Relates to Commensurable Magnitudes.*

Across the hall, the library dedicated to general literature included two quite different titles, penned by his alter ego: *Alice's Adventures in Wonderland* and *Through the Looking-Glass and What Alice Found There.*

Despite the popularity of his fantasy works and the obscurity of his scholarly tomes, Dodgson shunned the name of Lewis Carroll, refusing even to acknowledge anyone who addressed him thus and returning, unopened, all correspondence bearing the pseudonym.

His friends knew him as Dodgson, he was introduced to strangers as Dodgson, and "Dodgson," not "Carroll," he insisted, would be inscribed upon his memorial stone.

Today, Dodgson dined alone at a table overlooking the garden. He wondered where Holmes was and whether he had learned anything more about Pritchard's murder.

He thought about the snoozer's tool he had first seen protruding from the chest of a dead man. It wasn't a squeamish thought. Medicine fascinated him. He studied it. In '57, he had gone to Barts to witness a leg amputation, and he had recently purchased an articulate skeleton.

Over and over, he rehearsed the evidence, trying to tie it together as he'd heard the barristers do time and again at the Oxford Assizes. But the case he now considered seemed to make no sense.

Dodgson moved to the library and sank down into a stuffed leather chair. A flunkey handed him the *Times*.

Alderman Sir Sydney Hedley Waterlow elected the new Lord Mayor.

Widespread cholera outbreak in India.

Henry Stanley's apologetic for Livingstone.

At a table opposite the fireplace, the mysterious Phileas Fogg sat stoically while his whist partner, Gauthier Ralph, ran out of trump and Andrew Stuart and Thomas Flanagan took the hand.

No one knew for certain just who Fogg was, where he came from or how he lived. All anyone could be sure of was that he was regular. You could set your watch by his comings and goings, and some did.

Gentleman burglar strikes again. Baffles police.

"Anything interesting, old man?"

Dodgson looked up from his paper to see Dr. Bensley Lawrence, the archaeologist renowned for his discoveries in the Philistine temples of Ashkelon.

"Allow me to present my good friend, Monsieur Jules Verne. He has come all the way from Amiens to pick my brains for what he hopes will be his magnum opus, an ambitious work he's calling T*he Discovery of the Earth*.

"While the scientist in me respects his scholastic endeavors, the adventurer, I'm afraid, is a hopeless captive of his *Journey to the Centre of the Earth*, *From the Earth to the Moon*, and *Twenty Thousand Leagues Under the Sea*."

Dodgson stood and shook their hands in turn.

"Bonjour, Mssr. Dodgson, I am also the admirer, *non*?

"Years ago, when my son Michel was seven, we would walk along the beach of Crotoy and I would ask him, 'Would you tell me, *s'il vous plait*, which way I ought to go from here?'

"A big grin would spread across his face for he knew and loved our game. Then, looking up at me he would say, 'That depends a good deal on where you want to get to.'

"'I don't much care where,' I would say, shrugging my shoulders.

"Then Michel would shrug his little shoulders in the same way and answer, 'Then it doesn't matter which way you go.' And we would both double over laughing at your fine jest."

"Please excuse me, gentlemen," said Lawrence, "but may I suggest that we find a fourth for whist so that we can at least sit down and sip whiskey while you proceed to gratify one another's fragile literary egos?

"Hullo, there's young Hartley. I say, Hartley, come and join us. We're just sitting down to cards." Handsome and accomplished, Richard Hartley was generally liked at the Reform.

Introductions made all around, Dodgson was paired with Verne, and the foursome sat down to whiskey and cigars.

Conversation for the first hour meandered comfortably along familiar paths of politics, economics and science, as conversations usually do among men.

"It has long been my concern," said Verne, "that science may prove to be the proverbial tiger that man dares not dismount. We ride confidently upon its muscled back, yet do we not fear deep inside that it must one day grow hungry and devour us?"

"If Christian doctrine declares that a man is born predisposed to sin," said Dodgson, "science merely provides him with more efficient weapons and wants only a motive and circumstances to be employed for some evil.

"Consider, for example, the so-called Gentleman Bandit who's been in our papers for the past several weeks.

"Until last night, when he apparently burglarized the home of Sir Arthur Bellingham, he had always acted the gentleman. He came in and did his work without making a mess. Actually, he was becoming a bit of a folk hero among the poor, who love nothing more than the sight of the rich losing their pretty baubles. Suddenly, though, the benign and gracious gentleman became a vicious killer. Do you say that brutality and murder were always part of his nature?"

"I think they always have lurked in us and in our fathers —even in whole societies and cultures," said Lawrence. "I agree that technology is not the cause of this evil but rather its pawn. Fire is discovered, and one man cooks a meal while another burns down the first man's house. When iron is discovered, one man puts venison on the table while another raises an army."

"You speak of a good man along with the evil one," interposed Hartley. "I say circumstance is the villain. Perhaps we are born evil, but then education makes us good. We are taught to be decent, to obey laws and help those who are less fortunate. Then, a circumstance arises and the good man makes a mistake, an honest error in judgment, and suddenly his life is in ruins. Should not whatever he does to protect himself from such ruin be held virtuous?"

"You sound like my Captain Nemo, my friend," said Verne. "He too confused virtue with self-righteousness. Pleading the cause of man, he destroyed man to justify Nemo."

Suddenly aware that his voice had been rising, Hartley swallowed the last of his whiskey and smiled.

"You are correct, of course, monsieur. Perhaps I was feeling a little compassion for our Gentleman Burglar. I confess that I too had begun to admire his exploits, if only for his boldness and style.

"And now, gentlemen, as I see this hand has given our opponents the winning point, I must ask you to excuse me."

And without another word, Hartley bowed and left.

Moving to more comfortable chairs around the fireplace, The remaining three continued to discuss the exploits of the Gentleman Burglar. Dodgson described his experiences at the manor with Holmes.

"The disturbing thing," said Lawrence, "is that every victim has been a member of this club."

"What?"

"In fact, the police have been here several times asking questions. I know the other chaps, all except Bellingham. Heard of him, of course, but never met the fellow."

"Have they anything else in common?" asked Verne, who seemed unusually interested in our local crime.

"Only that each burglary appeared to have inside assistance. But that just makes things more baffling. While it is hardly uncommon for a newly employed domestic to walk off with a bit of plate or for a silly girl to open the front door for some sweet-talking cracksman, no one could have pulled off so many jobs in such a short time across such a vast area. But the police cannot imagine any other way the Gentleman Burglar could have committed the crimes so flawlessly."

Dodgson recalled the discussion with Sir Arthur following the murder. Holmes had asked whether anyone was aware of Bellingham's invitation to Buckingham and that his wife intended to wear the jewels. And Bellingham said that no one knew except his wife and "a few of the fellows at the club."

"Lawrence," said Dodgson suddenly, "please introduce me to the other four members whose homes were robbed."

"Certainly, but why?"

"Please come with us, Mssr. Verne. You may discover an idea for a new adventure."

Armitage, Wedmore and de Vere were easily located, but Joseph Crawley was not at the Reform, being abed, recovering from a case of brain-fever caused by the shock of the burglary.

Dodgson asked each in turn the question Holmes had asked Bellingham. Then, he asked them to try to recall the names of everyone they had talked to about their jewels. Wedmore answered for Crawley, having been present when Crawley boasted of "stealing" a consignment of gems from a new auctioneer in Sheffield.

At the end, several names were common to every list. So Dodgson excused himself and hurried back to Dulwich where Sir Arthur narrowed the field to one name.

* * * * *

Dodgson pulled up in front of Hartley's apartments just in time to see the young man step into a hansom.

He followed and watched as Hartley's cab made three stops. The first was on Old Bond Street, where he merely sat outside and waited.

* * * * *

A steady line of cabs discharged silk-hatted passengers at the Threadneedle Street entrance to the Bank of England.

Inside, a pale-faced gentleman of about forty years of age, tall and handsome, with light hair and whiskers, walked to the table of the Principal Cashier and stood behind a stooped, elderly gentleman who meticulously counted out three shillings and sixpence. The silver and copper coins blushed among the shining sovereigns, gold ingots and packets of bank-notes on the Principal Cashier's table.

"Three and six," announced the gentleman.

"Three and six," repeated the Principal Cashier.

"You may count it," said he.

"That won't be necessary, sir."

"There must be no mistake. Finance is very precise, you see. You're too young to know that well, but it is, I can tell you. Every jot and tittle in its place, or do you know what happens, sir? You make an error, nothing malicious, not a greedy error that is not really an error but a falsification, no. You do something careless because you've done it so

46

many times before and you don't understand how precise finance is."

He took up the coins again and counted them out slowly for the Principal Cashier.

"Three and six," said he.

"Three and six," repeated the Principal Cashier.

Looking again at the stack of coins, the old man turned and left the paying-room, continuing to recite his lesson as though the Principal Cashier was escorting him to the doors.

The Principal Cashier set aside the old man's coins, took up his pen and registered the deposit.

When he finally looked up again, the pale-faced gentleman was gone.

Outside, on Threadneedle Street, the pale-faced gentleman entered the waiting cab, his right arm pressed tightly against a thick packet inside his coat.

The second stop was at the Post Office on Rochester Row where the man posted the packet.

Finally, the two men continued to a haggard East End pawn shop called "Solomons."

The death of Holmes

SKEWES BROUGHT a temporarily abandoned dray around to the alley behind the pawnshop. Rasch and Pruitt swore as they carried their awkward bundle and pitched it onto the rough boards. Even through the canvas, Holmes could smell the reek of the vehicle's customary freight.

Down the narrow alleys behind Houndsditch, across Aldgate and along Minories, the cart rumbled toward the docklands.

An hour earlier, Limehouse workers had begun to return to their jobs.

Stern and sullen, some of them. Others, loudly jesting and laughing at the same things they'd laughed at the day before and would laugh at again tomorrow.

Dark-skinned seamen in blue coats returned to their shrouds and halyards.

Taut-muscled dockworkers and broad-shouldered warehousemen went back to their hauling and hoisting—seventy thousand pipes of wine in this storehouse, twenty thousand hogsheads of tobacco in that.

Porters and touters. Costermongers and vendors. Gritty, barefooted children running amongst the carters and clerks. Negroes, Lascars, Portuguese.

Last night, after many pints and little distraction, the tenants of Limehouse beat each other's brains out. Then, sodden and broken, they staggered back to their houses and dependably arose again before daybreak to turn the wheels of commerce.

"This'll serve, mates," said Rasch in a raspy whisper, as though he'd just entered a church and spotted a pair of gleaming candlesticks unattended.

Two pairs of boots clattered onto the stones. Two pairs of hands tugged at the canvas and pulled it up over the side of the dray. Two men carried their long bundle to the end of the pier, dropped it into the river and watched as it pitched briefly, then sank.

* * * * *

Dodgson did not wait for anyone to come out of the pawnbroker's but took the next train back to Christ Church, totally unprepared for what he found.

"Good God!"

"You're back," said Holmes, awakening. "What o'clock?"

"Half past seven. But what … how …?"

"What day?"

"Monday, but really, Holmes …"

50

As he struggled to regain his wits, Holmes recounted what had happened since they had parted at the Egyptian Hall.

"After I made my way back, I stopped by to tell you that I was going to sleep and would meet with you this evening. But as you see, I was seduced by the warmth of your fire and the comfort of your rug before I could return to my rooms."

"Yes, yes, but you've left out the most important part of your story. How did you escape drowning?"

"I'm sorry, old fellow. Be patient and allow me a hot bath and dry clothes. We'll meet back here and I'll explain all."

An hour later, Holmes returned to find the sideboard laid with hot meats and bread, pastry and wine.

"You asked how I escaped the Thames," he said, as the two sat down to table. "Do you recall the Davenport brothers and their notorious spirit cabinet?"

"Certainly" said Dodgson, ignoring his meal.

"Maskelyne exposed the trick. The brothers, William and Ira, allowed themselves to be tied hand and foot and placed in the end chambers of a three-room cabinet.

"In the centre chamber were loose instruments which, after all three doors were secured, suddenly began to sound and come flying out of the open top of the cabinet as though thrown by mischievous spirits. When the doors were opened again, the brothers were still securely bound.

"In 1864, when Maskelyne was still an amateur magician, the Davenports appeared in Cheltenham. The performance was held in the afternoon, so the brothers asked that the blinds be drawn to shut out the light. Maskelyne had arranged with a friend to open one of the blinds at his signal. When he did, everyone saw Ira untied and manipulating the instruments."

"Then the Davenports were actually escape artists who could quickly slip out of the ropes and back again?"

"Precisely," said Holmes, striking the table with his knife. "And that is how I escaped what was to be my watery grave.

"Admittedly, I am not an escape artist. But I recalled that crossed wrists, uncrossed after they are tied, provide enough slack to work the hands free.

"I tested the principle during my ride in the dray. It was hard going and left rather nasty burns on my wrists as you can see. But finally, at the bottom of the Thames and with the invaluable assistance of a sharp penknife, I was able to escape—although I must say, Dodgson, I nearly lost all hope of reaching the surface before my lungs burst. Now I perceive that you are about to burst with your own tale"

With the tedious detail of a scientist, Dodgson recounted his day—from Miss Kitchin's arrival to his thoughts on the train as he returned to Oxford—noting the curious coincidence of both of their trails leading to Solomons' pawnshop.

"What do you make of Hartley?"

"Filtering out the irrelevant points of your account," said Holmes, "if you'll forgive my expressing it thus, we are left with what can only be a blackmail victim."

"And just how do you deduce that?"

"The man's conversation. Defensive and personal. His expressions and gestures during the discussion about good and evil and the weakness of mankind strongly suggest that he was speaking of his own situation. And they were confirmed by the large bank withdrawal and the posting of the thick envelope, obviously filled with the notes. Certainly, these errands were in his mind at the club.

"But money is not his only payment to the blackmailer. His name on every one of your lists implicates him in the Reform Club burglaries as well.

"Engaged in casual conversation with his fellow members, it would be quite easy for him to obtain information concerning their valuables and the efforts they have made to protect them, then pass it off to the blackmailer who in turn passes it on to the burglar.

"And Solomons?" asked Dodgson.

"Undoubtedly the fence, inasmuch as some members of his race enjoy an excellent reputation for their skill with gems and precious metals. While seemingly unconscious in the back of his shop, I learned that a man named Strand is the owner of the curious murder weapon and is probably the second burglar who entered Bellingham's last night.

"Perhaps our friend Strand has fallen out of favor with his chums. Solomons was quite willing—believing me to be a plainclothes officer from Scotland Yard—to allow me to locate this fellow and charge him with murder. But because Solomons's cronies had foolishly led me to his shop, he was forced to have me murdered rather than risk my connecting him to Strand and the rest of this mysterious business.

"And so, to bring everything together, Dodgson, we began with what Inspector Jenkins believed to be a simple murder committed during a common burglary. We then discovered the identity of the second burglar who entered the library last night at Bellingham's. And we learned that a gang of jewel thieves, including a blackmailer, is trying to do away with him.

"Naturally, we may have uncovered nothing more than a family dispute. But I sense there is more to it than that, perhaps a great deal more.

"I feel a strange presence in all of this, as though there is some kind of malevolent puppet master lurking behind the curtain, pulling the strings of these deadly marionettes.

* * * * *

Tuesday morning, during breakfast in Dodgson's rooms, Holmes opened the *Times*.

"Dodgson! The Old Lady's been robbed!"

"What? Impossible! It's never been done."

"It was only a matter of time before someone violated that childlike trust that kept her from positioning neither grate nor guard between her gold and a pair of clever hands.

"The paper says someone simply picked up a packet of £55,000 in bank-notes and walked out. The theft wasn't even noticed until the five o'clock accounting.

"Ha! Listen to this: 'The bank's principal cashier told police that earlier in the day a gentleman stood for a few minutes at his counter and then disappeared without making a transaction. The man's description matches that of a former convict named James Strand who was convicted of forgery in 1850 and served twenty years in Dartmoor.'

"Does anything strike you as odd about this?"

"It's curious that a successful cracksman and hotel thief would risk robbing the Bank of England in broad daylight."

"Something more than curious, I should say. It appears absolutely scripted, as though someone had written the plot, cast the players and moved the drama along, scene by scene."

"But who and why? What could Strand have possibly done to bring down such wrath upon his head?"

"Only he can tell us that, I'm afraid," said Holmes. "And to find him, we shall need to pay a visit to my friend, Pruitt."

Hunt for Strand

PRUITT CONDUCTED his business from a side stall at the Nag's Head and earned not very much less by forging testimonials, responses to enquiries and glowing letters of introduction, than he once earned by clerking at Merton, Cranwell & Rudd, attorneys-at-law, the Temple. On average, Pruitt could count on ninepence for a plainspoken letter, a few shillings for a certificate or petition and half a crown for the signature of a person of noteworthy reputation. Beggars, vagrants and cadgers were his clients. And many travelled an inconvenient distance to London to secure his services, for Pruitt, when he was sober, could be brilliantly inventive.

Today, he was sober and putting the finishing touches on a begging letter for a company of former dockworkers posing as shipwreck survivors and meaning to live for a time off the kindness of country farmwives.

Tomorrow, Pruitt would be drunk.

* * * * *

Holmes knew that neither Pruitt nor his two cronies were likely to recognize him as the man they drowned in the Thames, and he devised a way to return with Dodgson to the lodging house and interview the screever.

They took Sir Arthur into their confidence, since, at their

request, he had asked Scotland Yard to guide them as well as a small group, including a photographer and a young historian, through the deadly warrens.

Such tours were not uncommon. Charles Dickens toured several rookeries with the formidable Inspector Field, and a year later saw the signing of the Common Lodging House Act that helped shut down many of the meaner tenements.

Dodgson warmed immediately to the opportunity to conduct such a rare photographic study. And that night they wound their way through, occasionally entering a dim, low-ceilinged public house or pausing when a bullseye lamp startled a haggard face.

"What! You are there, are you, Tom Gower?" growled the detective. "What are you creeping around here for?"

And Tom Gower or young Lynch or Bill Slaine would listen humbly, then slink back into the darkness and resume his mischief.

The small party continued thus until, shortly after one o'clock, it reached the lodging house. While the visitors warmed themselves before the fire, the detective addressed half a dozen men and women, among whom were Rasch and Pruitt. The room tensed each time Dodgson's flash powder exploded.

None seemed to recognize Holmes, and Pruitt flinched

when he came alongside and slipped a note into his hand. He read it, then followed Holmes outside.

"You said you'd make it worth my while. What do you want with me?"

"I want to save you from transportation at best, a walk up the gallows at worst. Don't you recognize me, Pruitt?"

"How do you know my name? Who are you?"

"I'm the bloke wot said 'eed pick 'is teeth with the snoozer's tool if that weasely cove didn't think it was worth a bloody shilling—the one you sewed into a sheet of filthy canvas and dumped into the Thames."

"That wasn't me," he nearly shouted, his eyes open wide. "I didn't throw you in the river. I only helped Rasch carry you out and rode along on the cart. Skewes and Rasch. They're the blokes that did you. I swear."

"It's a jury you'll have to convince if you're caught, not me. But you needn't be alarmed. I have come for neither vengeance nor justice, unless your loyalty to your friend inside should prove stronger than your affection for your skin."

"What do you want?"

"I want Strand. You know where I can find him."

"I know him, but I can't tell you where he is. He's gone.

None of us knew Jim was marked until we heard it from the old man, and we still don't know why. So, after we came back from the river, I went to Jim and told him he'd been marked and that he better hoop it up to Edinburgh and dig in. He cracks cribs up north when things become too hot here."

"And did he go then?"

"He grabbed his kit and was on the next train."

"And that was in the morning?"

"Right after Rasch and Skewes thought they'd killed you and got their pay from Solomons."

"Where can we find Strand in Edinburgh?"

"You can't. At least, no way I know of. Nobody could now. He won't stick his head up for anything but a quick, easy job."

* * * * *

Back at Tom Quad, Holmes and Dodgson went over Pruitt's story.

"He'll not allow himself to be found, Dodgson. He'll have to be flushed and trapped."

"What about using Hartley? If he is being blackmailed for information, we could make something up for him to pass on to Strand. Lord Brian Douglas is an acquaintance of mine. I've visited his home and photographed his family. I'm certain he'll be willing to help when he knows what is at stake. I could take you, posing as his brother or cousin or such, as my guest to the Reform.

"Then, I can introduce you to Hartley and let him draw you into talking about your brother's wealth. If the prize tantalizes, Hartley might pass it along, and we'll be there when Strand shows up."

"You know, my friend," Holmes said with a wry smile, "it was that kind of mind that conjured up those inscrutable puzzles and mazes of yours that first attracted me. Let us proceed."

The next afternoon, young Hartley was invited to join them for lunch, during which time he learned of a fine prize in Scotland which would, several days hence, be vulnerable.

By half past twelve, Holmes and Dodgson were aboard a railway carriage heading north.

* * * * *

Arriving at Waverley Station, Dodgson wanted to stretch a bit, and Holmes saw no objection since their rendezvous with James Strand was set for Thursday evening. They walked down Princess Street, along the Mound and through the peaceful cemetery at Greyfriars.

There, John Gray's faithful Skye terrier, Bobby, lay buried

in a fresh grave beside his beloved master—at whose plot he had mourned for fourteen years.

They walked the halls of Edinburgh Castle and visited the royal apartments in which Mary, Queen of Scots, gave birth to James I. On the battlements among the cannon, Holmes lit his pipe, and they watched the sun settle over the firth.

"You know what King James would say to that?" asked Dodgson.

"To what?"

"Your pipe. He called smoking 'a custom loathsome to the eye, hateful to the nose, harmful to the brain, dangerous to the lungs, and in the black, stinking fume thereof, nearest resembling the horrible Stygian smoke of the pit that is bottomless.'"

"Reason enough for Guy Fawkes to pile 30 barrels of black powder under Parliament with the intent of returning his boorish majesty to Scotland," said Holmes.

The red deepened in the sky, and they started toward Castle Street where the restless ghosts of Rob Roy and Ivanhoe haunted the lengthening shadows.

Lord Douglas was a man of two score, ten and six. Tall, lean and erect, he had the bearing of a highland officer.

Introductions were made, and after a late supper, the three

men gathered in the study to work out final details for the next day's adventure.

Resurrection

"I CAN'T IMAGINE what's happened to Holmes," said Dodgson testily. "He left this morning before anyone arose, and I haven't heard from him all day."

"Perhaps your friend feels he's done his part and is leaving us to spring the trap," answered Lord Douglas. But neither man believed that his disappearance was that simple.

Detective Tidd, dispatched to Edinburgh with a warrant immediately after the bank robbery, said nothing. Nor did MacDonald, the local officer assigned to ensure that the Crown's fugitive was transported safely back to London.

The lamps had been extinguished, and the rest of the household was gone.

Dodgson wished now that he hadn't been quite so liberal in his attempt to make the prize attractive. Telling Hartley that no one would be home until the next day gave Strand all night to carry out his mission. What if he didn't come until dawn and they had to sit stiff and silent the whole time?

Suddenly, the front door swung open and a torch played on the walls of the front hall. The four men tensed. A pistol was cocked.

"An ominous sound to greet a friend. I trust you won't

fire before you sight your target."

"Holmes! What do you mean by coming in this way? You might have spoiled the whole plan."

Someone hastily lit the gaslights.

"And what's all this?" asked Lord Douglas, staring past me at two uniformed policemen and a manacled seaman.

"Allow me to introduce to you Mr. James Strand."

* * * * *

Holmes apologized for his dramatic entrance and, while MacDonald escorted Strand and Tidd to the train station, explained in detail how the burglar came to be in chains rather than making his way toward their carefully baited trap.

"As we walked through the city after our arrival, I was struck by the complete absence of effective concealment. Edinburgh is a commercial town, every street lined with shops and houses. Where, I asked myself, would a man hide if he is trying to prevent his former friends from cutting his throat? He would be unlikely to try to conceal himself as a shop clerk in the bustle of St. Stephen Street or as a bank cashier amidst the business of St. Andrew Square. So, I looked beyond the city.

"Atop Castle Rock, as Dodgson looked across the rooftops, I gazed farther west toward the docklands at Leith.

Perhaps a stevedore. No, the risk is far too great of being recognized by one of the cut-throats that do business with Solomons and his thieves.

"Beyond the docks were the fishing villages on the firth. Strand would be quite invisible there, perceived as another fisherman, on the boat all day, fading at night into the stupor of a crowded pub.

"I determined to leave before dawn and learn whether an Englishman had arrived within the past couple of days seeking work. While confident that our little trap was well manned, I knew there was a chance that our rabbit might not take the bait.

So, before I went to the villages, I visited the offices of *The Scotsman* and examined the London newspapers as well. None carried anything which might be our message.

Either Hartley had become suspicious and failed to pass on the information to his blackmailer or we were wrong about the vehicle being used to alert Strand. But even if he had received the message, Strand might think it a trap set not by the police but by his gang.

"The morning wore on, and I found no lead.

"Early in the afternoon, I inquired at the fishmarket and learned that a middle-aged Englishman had signed aboard the *Williamina* recently. He would return with the other boats before sundown, they said, if I wanted to see him.

"I did, indeed.

"While I waited, I remembered that Strand had served a twenty-year sentence at Dartmoor.

"A virtual lifetime of penal servitude would leave him either broken or remarkably strong, the latter seeming the more likely, given his current occupation. In addition, his recent betrayal would make him alert and wary—a dangerous quarry to try to capture alone, even by surprise.

"Returning to Branksome Hall to fetch you, I risked losing him, for I could not tell whether he might yet take our bait. He may well have received the message, made some excuse not to go out on the boat today and be on his way here after all.

"Instead, I requested the services of the police at Leith, the two gentlemen you met earlier.

"I doubt that they would have accompanied me, however, had they not read about the Bank of England robbery and been assured that a Scotland Yard detective was waiting here, warrant in hand, to take his man back to London.

"Despite our efforts at concealment, Strand must have spotted their uniforms, for he immediately jumped to shore and bolted.

"Within moments, I was within reach. With a single move, I kicked his trailing foot toward the other, taking him down."

"Amazing, Holmes."

"Baritsu, my dear Dodgson—the third aggressive discipline the Squire insisted that I study during our family travels, in addition to fencing and fisticuffs."

"Did Strand tell you why his gang had turned against him?"

"He is, I am afraid, quite as much in the dark as Pruitt is. Nevertheless, I am convinced that he holds the answer, though he is clearly unaware of it. And I am just as certain that it involves a great deal more than a few sparkling gems. In the morning, we take the first train to London. Then, directly to Newgate."

* * * * *

A great stone sepulcher, Newgate Prison has stood silent and omnipotent for nearly seven centuries. A wretched nursery, it weans the innocent and the guilty from humanity's milk, raises them to scorn and violates every law of man and nature, then turns them out shattered, bitter or mad—else it ends their wretchedness upon the scaffold.

"Strand is in great danger, Dodgson," said Holmes after they had returned to his rooms. "We must see him tonight at all cost."

As they went over their plans, he thumbed through the *Newgate Calendar,* the prison's monthly bulletin of executions.

"Countless souls have walked through the debtor's door and stepped onto that dark apparatus with the tolling of St. Sepulcher's ringing in their ears," said Holmes as he read.

"Here's a cold February morning with 40,000 clogging the streets and balconies to see John Holloway and Owen Haggerty pay their due for the murder of John Cole Steele on Hounslow Heath. Alas, they did not die alone. While their bodies were being taken down, St. Bartholomew received the corpses of twenty-eight spectators who had been trampled by the frenzied crowd.

"And here's the poisoner, Catherine Wilson. Some still claim they saw the ghosts of her victims laughing on the scaffold as the hood was pulled down over her face."

Just then, their cab arrived, and they left for their meeting with London's most famous prisoner.

Newgate

HOLMES AND DODGSON walked up the four stone steps and through the heavy iron-spiked door of Newgate. Inside was a terrible silence.

Their voices echoed back and forth between the thick walls and faded as they felt their way along the close, uncertain corridors.

They were led to the visitors' room and signed their names in the book. On a shelf were displayed plaster casts of the heads of John Bishop and Thomas Williams, hanged December 5, 1831 for murdering a poor Italian boy.

Next-door, in the warders' lodge opening onto the Old Bailey courthouse, hung a collection of irons, two sets said to have manacled the infamous highwaymen Jack Shepherd and Richard Turpin.

Many twistings and turnings led them finally into the "glass house," a trophy of recent prison reforms. In this small room, a prisoner could now talk privately with his attorney and still be watched by the turnkey. Holmes and Dodgson sat down to wait for Strand.

The man brought to them, however, was so unlike the one they had seen in Edinburgh as to cause them to alert the warder to his mistake.

"No mistake. This is 'im wot pinched 'er Majesty's purse. E'll be in the salt box and topped before it snows, see if 'e ain't," said he as he closed the door.

Strand's eyes were dark and deep-set in his pale face, giving him the look of one already condemned. He sat, staring at something dark inside himself.

"Strand! Look at me," Holmes said sharply.

He obeyed mechanically.

"Do you know me?"

"I know you."

"Strand! Look at me and listen. Your life is not yet forfeit, but only you have the power to save it and unravel this devilish riddle. You've got to fight, man! We know you did not rob the Old Lady. Nor did you murder Robert Pritchard."

"Murder? No one said anything about murder. I've killed no one. What are you saying?"

Slowly Strand's color returned, as Holmes described the Bellingham burglary, the death of Sir Arthur's manservant and the nature of the murder weapon.

His eyes cleared and darted back and forth, as he tried to piece the words together.

76

"That was part of my cane, a tool to crack hotel rooms. But I swear that I lost that handle. I've never even been to Bellingham's house."

"That won't do, Strand," said Holmes, standing and walking to the door. "I will not help you if you lie to me.

"In fact, you did indeed come to Bellingham's that night, but Pritchard was already dead when you arrived. A message in the agony column of the newspaper told you about the jewels, where they were kept and when it would be safe for you to enter. And you did precisely as you were told.

"You planned to steal the diamond and ruby pieces and take them to Solomon's as you've done many times since your release from Dartmoor.

"But something went wrong. You cut a hole in the glass of the garden door, reached in and turned the lock. But the lock was not set. Nevertheless, the door would not swing open because it was blocked by a body. You were confused. Then, you heard the police arrive and fled.

"The morning the Bank of England was robbed, a screever named Pruitt came to your house and warned you that the members of your gang were out to kill you. He didn't know why, nor did you.

"He told you to leave the City immediately, which you did. In fact, you were on a train when the bank was being robbed and didn't even know it had happened, until I brought you down on the beach in Scotland and the local police told you the charge against you."

Strand's eyes were wide open, his jaw slack.

"I don't understand. How … ?"

"That's not important right now. We have little time to find out who is behind all of this. Who wants you dead, Mr. Strand, and why?"

"I have no idea. It's as much of a mystery to me, Mr. Holmes, as it is to you, although you seem to know so much that I can't think why you don't know that too."

"I don't, but I am going to. Now concentrate. I want you to tell me about your background. Begin with your forgery arrest. Omit nothing."

James Strand slumped in his chair, his hands lying loosely in his lap, his eyes gazing back in time.

"I once was a man with expectations, Mr. Holmes. My father began as a warehouse clerk but learned quickly and found favor with several businessmen. Eventually, he was able to purchase his own warehouse. He even purchased a merchant ship.

"Growing up on the Thames, I was accustomed to and thrived on the company of rough young men. We shared a wild spirit, I suppose. Nothing unusual in youth.

"One day a friend of mine introduced me to several men who had been quite successful forging bank notes. I didn't need the money, but the risk was exotic and excited me, so I threw in my lot with them.

"It wasn't long before the four of us were caught. My fault, really. They were clever enough, but I was involved with a girl, got drunk and boasted to her of our exploits. She wasn't the only girl I was seeing, and she found out about the others. She was furious and, out of spite, turned me in. Accused of being tied in with us and threatened with prison herself, she turned Queen's evidence."

"What then?"

"We had no defense. Dora—that was her name—had taken them to our rooms, and the police found everything … paper, pens and ink, sketches and enough queer to convince the dullest jury.

"I'll never forget the moment the verdict was read. I think I knew we'd be found guilty, but when I heard the words, my knees buckled and I nearly fainted.

"The walk back to Newgate was the longest of my life. Beneath my feet, under the passageway leading from the Old Bailey, were the bodies of those who had been hanged and packed in quicklime, their initials cut into the rough stones. With every step, I thought how near I had come to the same gibbet, how miserable their lives had been before the final day and how baneful mine would be for the next twenty years. That misery was not long in coming and far worse than I then imagined.

"Silence was the rule during the first year of confinement. No man was allowed to speak to another. We were strictly segregated.

"My stone cell was more of a cave than a room. It was two strides wide and three in length. The roof was only a foot above my head.

"In one corner of my cell was a water closet seat and, in the wall adjacent, a tap beneath which was fastened a bright copper basin which I had to keep highly polished.

"A small table held a Bible, Prayer Book and a copy of *Hymns, Ancient and Modern*. Affixed to the wall above were copies of the rules and dietary. Cope was governor of Newgate then; I was prisoner Z781.

"I had read, of course, of the prison reforms and the reconstruction, but I saw no evidence of any comforts nor knew any during the two decades that I enjoyed the Queen's hospitality.

"The third night of my imprisonment, a man named Watts hanged himself in the infirmary. I determined to keep my life and my sanity if it could be done. I was not a strong man then. I was sick in body and mind. I couldn't sleep or keep any food down.

"For the most part, we sat in our cells and were made to pick the hardened tar out of old ship's ropes.

"It was winter, and my hands were ever raw, stiff and bloody. The cold was maddening. We could never get warm. The heat from the ward-fires went straight up to the roof. We spent as much as fifteen hours a day in total darkness. A candle was the only source of heat. Our clothes were thin as paper and the vermin-infested blankets of no use.

"I don't see where this is getting us, Mr. Holmes. What has my imprisonment got to do with the Bank of England or Pritchard?"

"I don't know yet," said Holmes. "But I am certain that it holds the answer. And just as one retraces one's steps to locate a lost pocketbook, we must walk again the path you trod twenty-two years ago."

"Very well, then. There really isn't much more. One day was exactly like another. We worked when we had to, slept when we were told and ate what we could.

"I was not raised religious, Mr. Holmes. My father had no time for it, and my mother, who I'm told was a God-fearing woman, gave her life to bring me into this wretched world.

"But those religious books left in our cells—no doubt to cleanse our souls just as the silent segregation and endless labor were intended to chasten our behavior—kept me sane. Them and the ordinary.

"Most ordinaries are religious hirelings who bless you with a rebuke, flay you with the Good Book and read over your corpse if and when it becomes necessary. Their heavenly call is more of the jingle of £400 per annum than the voice of God, and they earn it with as few hours as possible in our company.

"Reverend Peter Morgan was not like any of them. Business hours were at a quarter to ten every morning, and I got my name on his list for rounds as often as I could.

"At first, it was just an excuse to talk to another human being. It made no difference to me whether it was a chaplain or a hangman. But there was something different about him. Not just his cloth or brogue or even the kindness he showed me. I wasn't a joey, a parson's man, but I became dependent on his being there, on seeing him and hearing him talk me up and remind me I was a man.

"Wiry and clean-featured, he had a ready hand and easy smile. He looked thoroughly out of place among the rascals and blackguards that pass through prison doors. But in later years at Dartmoor, I heard his name uttered with respect and a hint of longing. And there were others who went easier into eternity with the Scot at their side as the halter was pulled to.

"I was in the chapel the Sunday that Peter Morgan said an execution sermon for Jack Clews. I guess I heard those words again in my head a hundred times over the next nineteen years.

Bits and pieces of it straightened my back on the quarry gang at Dartmoor and preserved me when I was awash in self pity or aflame with rage.

"It wasn't your regular sermon, Mr. Holmes. Most ordinaries would have picked up the Stone Tablets if they could and pitched them down from the pulpit, like Moses from Sinai, to crack the skull of the bloke sitting alone on the condemned bench. But that day Peter Morgan preached a sermon he called, 'Behold therefore the goodness and severity of God.'

"He preached it right to Jack, as if Jack was the only one in the chapel and the pews weren't filled with prisoners and the galleries overflowing with gawkers and self-righteous do-gooders.

"'Jack,' said he, "You've heard enough, I'm bound, of God's wrath against sinners. Y'know how severe He can be in His holiness. But do y'know His kindness? Nae, ah can see you've never known a loving touch in your life.'"

"And then do you know what Reverend Peter Morgan did? He came down from his pulpit, walked over in front of old Jack, knelt down, put his hands on the prisoner's knees and looked up into his face. The rest of the sermon—and it was the shortest I've ever heard—was delivered from that spot right in front of Jack.

"'I remember when I was newly a believer," said he. 'Aye, I was not born a man of the cloth, y'know. Why, lad, ah drank hard, swore to perfection and spent more than a few coppers for soft company in the night. I lived like the devil and boasted of his kinship.

"'But it was a hollow boast. All bluster wi' no substance. Well, I'll not weary ye with the rest of that story. Let's say that a very kind and stubborn God finally caught up wi' me. And I was all worn out from running, so I gave in to Him.

"'What followed was all new t'me. I'd never prayed nor sung a hymn, never stepped inside of a church. And I had no one t'lead me. Everyone I knew was just like m'self. So, I knelt down in m'room an' folded my arms on the bed.'

"And Reverend Morgan folded his arms and laid them across Jack's legs."

"'And I put down m'head like this.'

"And he laid his head on his arms.

"You could hear a pin drop in that chapel. And the two of them stayed like that, Jack not knowing what to do with the ordinary on his knees in front of him like that. Finally, Peter Morgan got up and sat down beside Jack.

"'And d'ye know what happened then, Jack? It was as though I was kneeling at His feet, like He was sitting there on a great rock that had been my bed. And I felt the Lord Jesus wrap His arms around me like this.'

"And Reverend Peter Morgan put his arms around Jack and held him. At first, Jack was all stiff like he wanted to break loose. But then he started to weep, and his great shoulders shook. He put his head next to Reverend Peter Morgan's and let himself be held as though no one else was there. And I could see the back o' Peter Morgan shudder as he began to weep with him. And they sat there together, Peter Morgan's God caring for a prisoner like Jack, like the God I imagined my mother loving.

"The gallery was graveyard silent, listening to the ordinary saying over and over again, 'Behold therefore the goodness and severity of God,' as he looked into Jack's face."

"Jesus said, 'the Son of man came not to be ministered unto, but to minister, and to give his life a ransom for many.' For me, Jack, and for you. Aye, He's a holy God who cannot abide sin, and He's a just God who must have payment for our rebellion against His law.

"But He's also a good and kind God who 'so loved the world, that he gave his only begotten Son, that whosoever believeth in him should not perish, but have everlasting life.'

"You've been condemned by men, Jack. That verdict is

in, and you must pay the price tomorrow morning. God's verdict is in too. But He already paid the price for ye. And all that's wantin' is for ye to accept your pardon and give Him your allegiance.'

"I never saw Jack Clews again.

"By then I'd been at Newgate seven months. Five months later, I was transferred to the new Dartmoor gaol. And I swear I don't know which was worse.

"My cell was of corrugated iron. I was permitted to speak, but most conversations in that place were angry and bitter. The only hope we had was to learn enough from other prisoners so that we wouldn't get caught again once we got out.

"When I wasn't turning big rocks into little ones, I was studying. Chaplain Rickards' library had 4,000 volumes, including trade hand-books. I learned masonry, carpentry and a good bit about locks—crafts that made me a swell cracksman after I walked through the gate.

"That day finally came December 4, 1870. I received a suit of clothing from the Discharged Prisoners' Aid Society, was taken to the railway station at Horrabridge, given a convict's ticket for London and met at the other end by a man named Solomons."

"How did you come to know Solomons?" Holmes asked.

"Never met him in my life. But that wasn't unusual, Mr. Holmes. You make friends in prison, and those who get out first, if they're connected, often help others get set up when their turn comes. I never found out who my benefactor was, but I received a letter telling me that a Mr. Solomons would be waiting for me when I reached London.

"Solomons became my mentor. He taught me more tricks of the trade. Then, he sent me out with a seasoned cracksman until I got my legs under me. I learned quickly and was soon the best in his stable. There were seven of us that fetched gold and jewels for him."

"Did you make any enemies in prison?"

"I had few friends but no enemies that I know of."

"And after you were released?"

"I'm sorry, Mr. Holmes. Ever since Pruitt's warning, all I've done was try to think of who might have it in for me and who has the power to pull it off. I can think of no one."

"Very well, then, let's go back to your forgery conviction. Who were the others in your gang, and where are they now?"

"Well, one was a former bank clerk. His name is Edward Clifford. He lost his health in prison and was eventually transferred to Chatham. He was released a broken man and begs for his bread today. His mind is about gone. When I first encountered him after our release, I didn't recognize him nor he me.

"Pruitt was the second man. You met his younger brother at the public-house."

"The screever's brother was one of your gang?" Holmes asked, suddenly rigid, his eyes alert. "Does he bear you any grudge?"

"Oh, no. Quite the contrary. Will Pruitt is my age; the other two were older than us. Will and I grew up together on the Thames. And when we were convicted, he was with me at Dartmoor. I helped him once when another inmate attacked him in the quarry. He feels a debt. No, he didn't even blame me for our getting caught. Said we all knew the risks. It just fell out bad for us. That's why the younger Pruitt came to warn me that day. We're all three chums.

"Will's working on the docks now. Married and lives in Limehouse. Happy to be out and one of the few to turn to honest work."

"And the third?"

"Moriarty was the leader. Michael Moriarty. Brilliant fellow. Furious at being caught. Would certainly have killed me if he could, but he couldn't possibly be behind all this."

"How can you be certain?"

"He's dead. Died in Portsmouth after about three years. Stabbed, I heard. I don't know much more than that."

"I say, I wonder if he's any relation to Professor James Moriarty," said Dodgson. "Wrote a brilliant treatise on the binomial theorem that earned him the mathematical chair at a small university in the west of England. Melford, I think it was. I have a copy of his book, *The Dynamics of an Asteroid*. A masterful work.

"Some dark rumors about him, though. I heard he finally resigned and set up here in London as a private tutor who prepares men for entrance examinations into the officer corps and readies officers for promotion."

"I believe Moriarty did have a son named James, three sons actually," Strand said. "Would have been about six when we were arrested."

Suddenly, Holmes jumped to his feet.

"Good show, Dodgson!" he exclaimed. "We begin there. You may have discovered the key to unlock this mystery. Stout heart, Strand.

"Gaoler! Let us out!"

Moriarty

HAVING EASILY LOCATED the West End residence of Professor James Moriarty, Dodgson made an appointment to visit this fellow academic and renowned mathematician.

When Holmes learned that Moriarty would be away until he was to meet with Dodgson, he decided to precede him with an unannounced visit. Moriarty's housekeeper, believing Holmes to be a student prospect, gladly let him into the study to wait.

Only one thing was remarkable about the room. Behind the writing desk hung a painting titled *La Jeune Fille á l'Agneau* depicting a young woman resting her head on her hands. Holmes recognized immediately the delicate brush of Greuze and recalled reading that his painting had fetched £4,000 at the Portalis sale in 1865. A curious acquisition on the salary of a £700 per annum professor.

Holmes examined the rest of the study, including the contents of the desk, but found nothing to identify Moriarty with any occupation other than that of an academic.

Yet, as he left, he had a strong feeling that he had missed something. He was certain that he had examined everything in the room. Then, he realized that it was something *not* in the room that troubled him.

"How did you find him?" asked Holmes.

"Brilliant, charming and cordial," said Dodgson. "He has a soft, precise fashion of speech. Yet, it made me quite uncomfortable. I can't say just why."

"Perhaps he was too brilliant and charming?"

"That's it. He reminded me of a student who has secured the questions before the examination. All the answers came easily and without thinking, as though the whole dialogue had been scripted and thoroughly rehearsed."

"Yes. We will do well to learn more about James Moriarty. You focus your inquiries on the academic world, and I will attend to the professor."

* * * * *

Returning to Moriarty's residence, Holmes was told that the professor was at the London Library in St. James Square, as was his daily habit.

When Holmes reached the library, he saw Moriarty sitting in an alcove of the Reading Room, apparently absorbed in study. In front of him were several sheets of paper on which he made occasional notations. Then, he folded the stop sheet and slipped it into the book, which he replaced on the shelf himself instead of leaving it for the librarian. Finally, he gathered the remainder of his notes and left.

If Moriarty is indeed involved in this business, Holmes wondered, in what way is he involved? He could not be directly active in any sinister dealings, or he would have left some trace. He had a brilliant and highly organized mind and the potential for greatness, but whether for great good or great evil, Holmes could not yet tell. Such a man was capable of anything.

If this Professor Moriarty was corrupt, he must be the genius behind it, not the one who executes it. Far from risking his security, he would remain many layers removed from the thugs, thieves and murderers who populate the great London underworld, as Holmes himself would be should his intellect be twisted to an evil purpose.

Holmes had already begun to follow him out when he stopped and turned back to the stacks.

He discovered that the book Moriarty had returned to the shelf was Virgil's *Aeneid*. Holmes removed it and found the folded paper Moriarty had inserted between its pages. He then made an exact copy and replaced it.

And now, he waited.

What Holmes had copied was a cipher, brilliant both in

complexity and simplicity. The professor merely wrote his coded message and left it in a book for someone to pick up after he was safely away. A child's game.

Holmes continued to keep his eyes on the book until a Teutonic-looking gentleman with bushy eyebrows and moustache began to make his way slowly along the bookshelves. He paused briefly, then reached out and removed Virgil, found the message and slipped it casually into his coat pocket.

Sherlock Holmes followed him up Regent Street and down Piccadilly to number 37 Brick Street. Twenty minutes later, the old scholar emerged and retraced his steps. Once again, he removed Virgil and replaced the folded paper. This new message Holmes copied after the messenger had left and returned to Oxford with his spoils.

* * * * *

For his part, Dodgson had learned that James Moriarty was born October 31, 1846 in the west of England, the son of Michael Moriarty who had indeed died in Chatham Prison in 1853.

"There were two other brothers," Dodgson said. "One pursued a military career; the other was a station-master not far from his childhood home. James Moriarty was a man of good birth and excellent education. The rumors that forced his resignation from Melford were vague and unproved but sufficient to cause people in the small university town to ask questions.

"These rumors did not follow him to London. Here, everyone, including Scotland Yard, considered Professor Moriarty to be a gentleman devoted to transforming young Englishmen into distinguished Army officers."

Finished, Dodgson leaned back in his chair and shrugged his shoulders.

"What do you make of these?" said Holmes, placing the two messages on the table in front of him."

Dodgson examined them briefly.

"A devilish cipher, he said. "Impossible to solve without the key."

"Quite so" said Holmes. "And I don't think the key to these will be easily discovered.

"I'm sure it's in the book he used, from the exact place where he placed the message. But there are thousands of possibilities on those two pages. I say, hand me down the *Aeneid*, will you? And get your copy from your rooms.

When he returned, Holmes said, "You see what you can make out of the left page. I'll study the right. Think like a mathematician and see if anything emerges."

For hours the two applied each word to the cipher. Then they returned to the top of the page and tried groupings of words, as the paper mountain rose and spread.

"Dodgson," said Holmes at last. "Perhaps Moriarty wasn't wearing his board and tassel when he selected the key. Perhaps he was wearing his master-criminal's cap. What does this sentence suggest?

> 'Had I a hundred tongues, a hundred mouths, a voice of iron and a chest of brass, I could not tell all the forms of crime, could not name all the types of punishment.'

"This sounds to me like just the kind of irony a mind like his would find irresistible. Help me with the passage. I'll go word by word; you start with phrases."

They scribbled furiously, encouraged by the fresh scent.

An hour passed.

"I've got it!" shouted Holmes, pounding the table. "The key is the first five words together. 'Had I a hundred tongues.' Writing it above the message and using the classic Adleman grid, it reads:

> Royal Sovereign plans in hand five hundred thousand pounds must sell immediately other buyers await your decision.'

"Then it gets rather queer, and the key no longer seems to work. Here, look at this." He handed Dodgson the paper which read: "

zweisellenundengedanke

"German, I believe," said Holmes. "The first four letters spell *swei*, the German word for *two*."

He took down the German dictionary and soon had the phrase divided out.

"'Swei Sellen und en Gedanke' 'Two souls with but a single thought.'

"Moriarty is giving the agent the key for the next message. He writes the key to the next cipher with each message. The librarian at the London Library is certainly a confederate, getting down a different book each time for Moriarty, then passing on the title to the courier when he comes to the desk for assistance."

We translated the agent's response:

"Will have the money by Wednesday. How do you want to make the exchange?"

"Excellent," said Holmes. "That gives us three days to make our plans. I am certain now that Moriarty is the mastermind behind the jewel thefts, at least one blackmail and probably many more of London's criminal activities.

"He apparently inherited his father's diabolical strain as well as his genius ... and has burned with hatred for James Strand for getting his father thrown into prison and for his subsequent death behind bars, unless I miss my guess. Yet, he held that hatred in check these two years since Strand's release while Solomons taught him his craft.

"Then, he meticulously set him up for the hangman, no doubt savoring every thought of Strand on the gallows.

"Pritchard was murdered in cold blood for the sole purpose of seeing Strand hang. Moriarty even went so far as to take an incredible personal risk to ensure his demise by robbing the Bank of England disguised as Strand.

"Despite his ruthless brilliance, there's a providential irrationality in this devil, Dodgson. The very genius and passion that makes him one of the world's greatest villains also makes him vulnerable. His arrogance will be his undoing.

"And we shall be ready."

Treason

"DO YOU KNOW what you've got here, Sherlock?" asked Mycroft.

Even in those early days, Holmes' older brother, Mycroft, was a highly-placed unofficial official in the British government. Not as lofty as he would be later in the century, of course, but still privy to the most sensitive information that is carried about in locked red dispatch cases at Windsor. Mycroft leaned back in his chair and gazed out of his office window, the fingertips of his hands lightly touching.

"A bit of espionage," said the younger Holmes. "That is why I have come to you. What can you tell me about something called Royal Sovereign?"

"Nothing. It's one of the Crown's most closely guarded secrets."

"Not as closely guarded as Her Majesty would like. The plans are in the hands of Professor James Moriarty, *en route* to Germany. I can, I believe, retrieve them for you and present you with both the traitor and the German agent. But I must know what I'm dealing with."

"I see," said Mycroft. This was certainly unexpected, but Mycroft showed no emotion. He sat quietly for several minutes.

Then, having thought it through, he proceeded.

"Very well. *HMS Royal Sovereign* is a warship. At least she will be one day. She's years away from the building stage. Once completed, however, her triple-expansion engines will carry her over the waves at better than fifteen knots with a range of nearly 5,000 miles. Her armor will be eighteen inches thick, and she'll be armed with a primary battery of four 13.5-inch guns, backed by 30 quick-firing guns. There's never been anything like her.

"*HMS Royal Sovereign* will be mistress of the seas. But England, not Germany or France, must stand at her helm.

"The plans detail the concept for her revolutionary armaments, and they are still in the safe. That's why they've not been missed. Your Professor Moriarty must have a copy —the only copy, I hope. But that means there is yet another traitor.

"I believe I know away to ferret him out."

"Remember, there must be evidence, Sherlock. We must be able to prove that the money and plans changed hands. I'll trust that to your ingenuity. And we must keep this highly classified. Not even the Yard must know the nature of those plans. In the wrong hands, this ship could lead a fleet that could put Britain in chains."

Holmes left Whitehall to find John Nevil Maskelyne.

* * * * *

The next afternoon, when Moriarty arrived at the London Library, he requested the assistance of the librarian and sat down in the alcove with a book and note paper. Again, he folded a sheet, placed it in the book and returned to his house.

Again, Holmes watched every move.

This time, Holmes replaced the message with his own, which had been ciphered with the key given in the previous communication. It told the agent to be at the Egyptian Hall on Wednesday evening. Maskelyne would be performing a new illusion, it said, and when the conjuror called for volunteers from the audience, both he and Moriarty were to go up. The exchange would be made in the safest place in London—before two hundred spectators.

Soon the old scholar came and faithfully delivered the message to the Brick Street house, returning within the hour with a response. Once again, Holmes substituted one of his own making, instructing Moriarty to come to the Egyptian Hall in disguise and volunteer to assist with the illusion. He knew that the drama and irony of betraying his country in sight of hundreds of Britons would prove irresistible.

* * * * *

"I'm blowed if I know why the Home Office wants to open it all up again. Like I told you before, Mr. Holmes, it's as clear as can be. It was James Strand, not some mystery burglar, robbed the Bellinghams and killed old Pritchard. It was Strand that walked out of the Bank of England with a packet of bank-notes without so much as a by-your-leave. And it's Strand who's going to hang for it. It's as obvious as Her Majesty's cap, God bless her.

"What ain't all that obvious is how you can think a gentleman like Professor Moriarty is guilty with not a single bit of evidence. And then you top it by saying he's going to commit treason in front of half of London during a magic show. If my orders hadn't come from the Home Secretary, well …"

Chief Inspector Horace Jenkins waved his arms and shook his head as he paced.

"Moriarty has taken great pains to present a clean image, Chief Inspector," said Holmes calmly. "I assure you that all will be made clear tomorrow night. Your officers will be ready to arrest Moriarty and the German agent as they leave the theatre?"

"They will. But I don't expect it's them two gentlemen that'll be leaving with their tails between their legs."

* * * * *

Dodgson was so caught up with the performance that he did not notice the empty seat beside him. Hearing his cue,

Holmes had left to join Maskelyne's assistants.

* * * * *

How many of you are visiting us here this evening from abroad?" Maskelyne asked. "Ah, a goodly number. Then welcome, ladies and gentlemen, to our little island.

"Actually, a good deal of our cherished culture has come from your countries. And one of the favorites among our children is a charming little puppet show introduced by our neighbors across the Channel.

"Punch and Judy originated in Paris. And they live in a portable stage just like this one (at this, two assistants rolled onto the stage a large, brightly colored puppet theatre with the curtains open and open cabinet doors revealing the interior).

Maskelyne bent down, entered the theatre and looked around inside, all within the full view of the audience.

"Mr. Punch, are you at home? Mrs. Judy?"

Maskelyne looked out at the audience and leaned on the puppet stage.

"Oh, I am so sorry. I am afraid they have seen my poor conjuring so many times that they may have tired of my company."

He exited the puppet theatre through the same cabinet doors.

"But we must have a demonstration for our visitors. Will two of my countrymen please help me make our guests welcome? I need good actors to take the places of Punch and Judy. Come, come, now. For England and the Queen, gentlemen. Ah, yes, thank you, sir. And you, sir. Excellent. Come right up here with me.

"Oh, I'm sorry, I should have chosen one of the ladies to play Judy. Well, that's all right. You'll be in costume, so no one will know. May we have two costumes, please?

"Fine. Now, sir, you don't mind playing Judy, do you?"

"Not at all," said the tall, elderly gentleman with the bald head and white side-whiskers.

"Good."

Both men stepped into brightly-colored costumes which fastened at the back and put on the huge papier-mâché heads of Punch and Judy.

"Excellent! Now, if you will both just step into your theatre. That's good, right around the back and in through the door. That's it."

The two walked around the back of the theatre and were seen to enter. Maskelyne closed the cabinet doors once they were inside.

"Are you all right?"

Punch and Judy nod.

"Good. Now, I'm sure you both know the script. We'll just show our friends a little bit and then let you out of your hot costumes. I'll narrate while you act it out. Are you ready?"

Punch and Judy nod.

"One day, Judy went shopping and left Mr. Punch to mind the baby."

Judy reached down, picked up a baby doll and handed it to Punch, then turned and ducked down. But when Judy left, the baby began to cry. Punch rocks and pets the baby, but the crying grows louder and more insistent.

"Oh dear, can't you make the baby stop crying, Mr. Punch?"

Punch looks at Maskelyne and begins beating the baby.

"No, no, Punch, what are you doing?"

Punch continues hitting the doll, then throws it out of the theatre just as Judy comes home.

"I say, you're in for it now."

Judy looks for her baby, then looks down from the stage and sees the baby on the floor. She reaches down and picks up a stick and starts hitting Punch.

"I warned you, Punch."

Punch takes the stick away and begins beating Judy.

"What are you doing, Punch? Stop it this instant!"

He hits Judy one mighty blow. There is a blinding flash of lightening and a billowing of smoke. The four sides of the theatre collapse outward and slam down on the stage. Punch and Judy have disappeared.

"Ladies and gentlemen and my dear visitors, I assure you that this is not what usually happens. I cannot imagine what happened to our Punch and Judy."

Screams from the balcony where Punch is seen hitting Judy with the slapstick.

"How did you get up there? Come down here this minute!"

Punch and Judy return to the stage to loud applause.

"Gentlemen, you were wonderful."

Turning to Judy …

"And sir, I promise that we'll let you be Punch next time."

Judy removes her head to reveal the German agent.

"I don't understand. I thought I put the whiskered gentleman in there."

"I'm here," says Punch, who removes his head to disclose the aforementioned gentleman.

The audience applauds and cheers even more as the agent and the whiskered gentleman return to their seats.

* * * * *

The German agent was the first to leave the Egyptian Hall. He struggled furiously while two constables held him and a third snapped on handcuffs.

Several minutes later, the elderly gentleman allowed himself to be taken without resistance. Holmes stepped up and dramatically removed the skin-cap and whiskers.

But the man in the disguise was *not* Professor Moriarty.

Winners and losers

After Holmes had finished his account of the Bellingham Case, he stretched, arose, returned to the window and looked out again at cloudy, sodden Baker Street, which clearly still reflected his mood.

"The devil is out there still, Watson," said Holmes. "He's slipped through my fingers several times since then. But the day of reckoning is coming."

"Who was the man in the disguise then?"

"One of Moriarty's henchmen, no doubt. The Professor undoubtedly grew suspicious at the last moment—whether because of the changed cipher or something else, I never found out.

"But I did manage to save the plans and capture the German agent. I had arranged with Maskelyne to pose as one of his assistants during the Punch and Judy illusion. Two others were dressed in identical costumes and switched places with them when they walked around the back of the puppet theatre.

The German agent and the man I thought was Moriarty dropped through a star trap onto a thick mattress where I met them and instructed them to exchange costumes, which the ciphered messages had told them to expect.

"He who I believed to be Moriarty left the plans in the pocket of his costume as he had been told, and the agent left the money in the pocket of his costume. In helping them change, I witnessed the entire transfer to which I later testified in court.

"I then led them up the back stairs to the balcony and gave them their instructions for the finalé.

"After the police had captured both men and I realized that Moriarty had sent one of his own men, I warned Chief Inspector Jenkins to put a double guard on him, because I knew Moriarty must have assured him that he would break him out of Newgate. And I had no doubt that the Professor would make good on his promise.

Jenkins did not believe me, and of course the false Moriarty disappeared the next day."

"And James Strand?" asked Watson.

"He was easily acquitted at his trial. The railway ticket-seller and the train conductor both testified that Strand was on his way to Edinburgh when the Bank of England was robbed. And my testimony concerning the glass dust and the murder weapon convinced the jury that there was a second burglar at the Bellingham house that night.

"As for the butler's murderer, several months after the trial, a ruffian was arrested in a public-house brawl. He was said to have been boasting to his mates how he had got away with several killings, including 'the bloke what robbed the Bank of England.' That night, he was found hanging in his cell. The police said it was suicide.

"After his acquittal, Strand went to America. Nearly two years later, Dodgson forwarded a post he'd received from a prison chaplain at San Quentin."

Holmes went to the bookshelf and retrieved a scrapbook. He leafed through and removed an envelope. He opened it and read the letter to himself, then handed it to Watson:

Dear Mr. Holmes,

> I am writing to you on behalf of Mr. James Strand. He told me of his acquaintance with you in England but was not certain where to reach you and instructed me to post this to the Rev. Charles L. Dodgson, Christ Church, Oxford, in the hope that he would see that you received it.

> I had occasion to spend Mr. Strand's last hours with him, and much of the time, he spoke of you and the great efforts you had made on his behalf when he stood in the shadow of the gallows in 1872. Having no family, he desired that you would know what had transpired since he left England.

Having heard of profits to be made in the west, he came to San Francisco where, with neither resource nor reference, he reverted to his old trade, which proved too lucrative to abandon.

One evening, while he was burglarizing the home of a prominent family on Nob Hill, the owner entered the room and discovered Mr. Strand. The man was armed and fired at Strand. He missed. But Strand returned a shot which found its mark.

It was to his credit that he did not flee but tried to help the owner, then surrendered peaceably to the police. Mr. Strand pleaded guilty to murder at his trial and was sentenced to be hanged October 27, 1874 in the yard of the county gaol on Broadway.

I climbed the steps with him. Because of the notoriety of the murdered man, a large crowd had gathered that morning to witness the execution. Mr. Strand had asked forgiveness of the family and seemed to be at peace.

Asked if he had anything to say before his sentence was carried out, Mr. Strand turned and looked into every face below. Then, he smiled and said, "Behold therefore the goodness and severity of God."

[Editor's Note: In 1873, Mssr. Jules Verne published *Around the World in Eighty Days*, based in part on the Bank of England robbery involving James Strand, which he learned of during his card game with Rev. Charles Dodgson. In Verne's story, the capture required 78 days, a chronological adjustment of the true case to accommodate his plot. Surprisingly, there was little publicity over Strand's arrest and virtually none announcing his acquittal. The embarrassment of officials at the Bank of England's was so great that, to this day, anyone inquiring about the robbery of 1872 is assured that it never occurred.]

The Author

THE AUTHOR OF the international bestseller, *Son of Hamas*, Ron Brackin has traveled extensively in the Middle East as an investigative journalist. He was in the West Bank and Gaza during the Al-Aqsa Intifada, on assignment in Baghdad and Mosul after the fall of Iraq, and more recently with the rebels and refugees of Southern Sudan and Darfur.

Ron is the author of other fiction and nonfiction books and has contributed articles and columns to publications that include *USA Today* and *The Washington Times*.

He was a broadcast journalist with WTOP-AM, the all-news CBS radio station in Washington D.C. and weekend news anchor on Metromedia's WASH-FM. And he served as a U.S. congressional press secretary during the presidential administration of Ronald Reagan.

www.ingramcontent.com/pod-product-compliance
Lightning Source LLC
Chambersburg PA
CBHW051255170626
46809CB00004B/1654